Philomena's
NEW GLASSES

Brenna Maloney

Photographs by Chuck Kennedy

VIKING

Philomena, Audrey, and Nora Jane were sisters.
Philomena was the oldest, by three seconds.
Audrey was the largest, by half a pound.
And then there was Nora Jane.

Philomena   Audrey   Nora Jane

Philomena had a problem. She had terrible eyesight.
A pair of glasses made everything better.

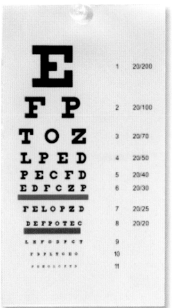

Before glasses

After glasses

Now she could see her sisters more clearly.

But as soon as Philomena got glasses,
Audrey got glasses, too.

Philomena disapproved.

"Audrey, you don't need glasses," she said.

"That's okay," said Audrey.

"I'll just wear them on top of my head."

This worried Nora Jane. She didn't need glasses, either.
But if her sisters were wearing glasses, then maybe she should, too.

Now all three sisters had glasses.
(Whether they needed them or not.)

BOUTIQUE

Not long after, Philomena bought a handbag.
It was a good place to keep her glasses.

Audrey decided she needed a handbag, too.
Not to put her glasses in, though.
Her glasses were always on top of her head.
She kept snacks in her handbag.

Philomena disapproved.
But the snacks were delicious.

Good grief, thought Nora Jane. Now I have to carry a handbag, too? My arms are too short for this. I'm not even a snacker.

Now all three sisters had glasses and handbags.
(With or without snacks.)

Not long after, Philomena thought that she might like to have a new dress to go with her new glasses and her new handbag.

Not to be outdone, Audrey rushed out
and found something to wear, too.

This is absurd, thought Nora Jane.
This dress makes my armpits itch. . . .

Now all three sisters had glasses and handbags and outfits.
(Itchy or otherwise.)

Nora Jane was miserable. She went to talk to her sister.

"Audrey," she said. "I don't need glasses. My arms are too short to carry a handbag. And this dress is itchy."

"Well," Audrey said, "my tutu is a little tight. But Philomena really needs her glasses. And I use my handbag for snacks."

But not everyone needs the same things.

And so it was decided that Philomena would keep her glasses.
Audrey would keep her handbag—for snacks.
Everything was fine . . .

. . . until Nora Jane got a necklace.

For my sisters, and for sisters everywhere.

VIKING

Penguin Young Readers Group

An imprint of Penguin Random House LLC

375 Hudson Street

New York, New York 10014

First published in the United States of America by Viking,

an imprint of Penguin Random House LLC, 2017

Copyright © 2017 by Brenna Maloney

LIBRARY OF CONGRESS CATALOGING-IN-PUBLICATION DATA IS AVAILABLE

ISBN: 9780425288146

Printed in China   Designed by Kate Renner   Set in Filosofia OT

1 2 3 4 5 6 7 8 9 10

No stunt doubles were used in the making of this book. Each guinea pig performed her own stunts, including hefty purse lifting, snug dress wearing, and extensive kale eating.

Deleted Scenes